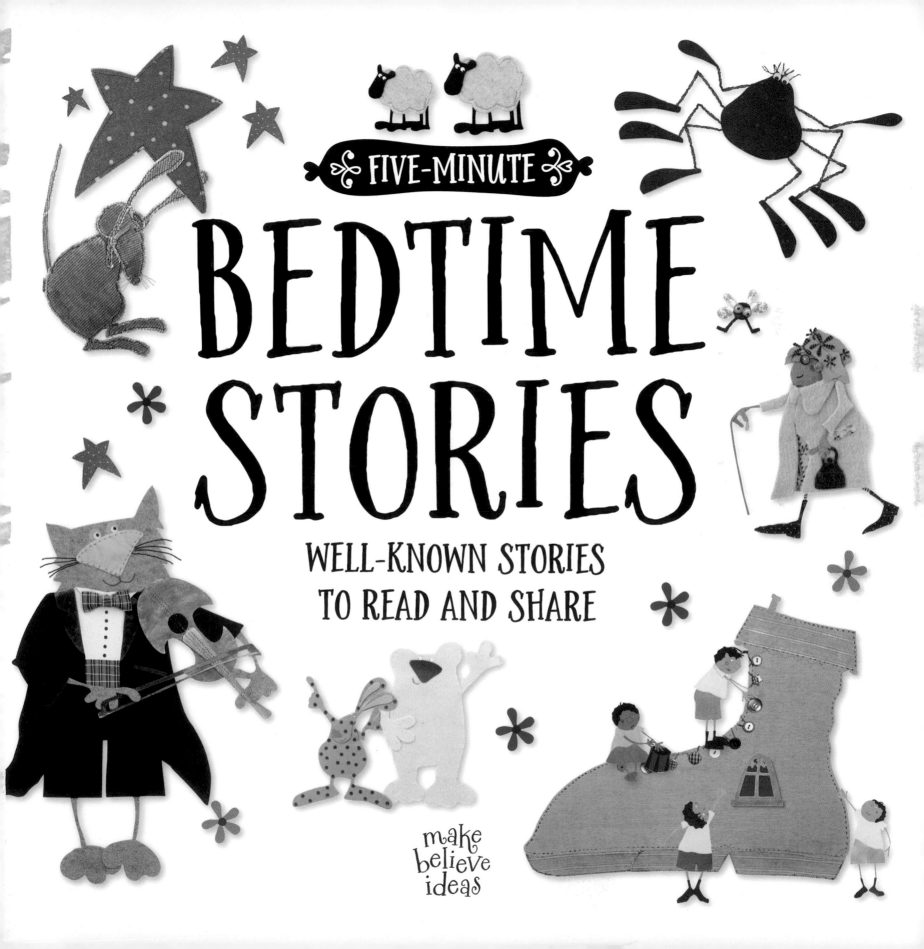

FIVE-MINUTE
BEDTIME STORIES

WELL-KNOWN STORIES
TO READ AND SHARE

make
believe
ideas

ILLUSTRATED BY KATE TOMS

CONTENTS

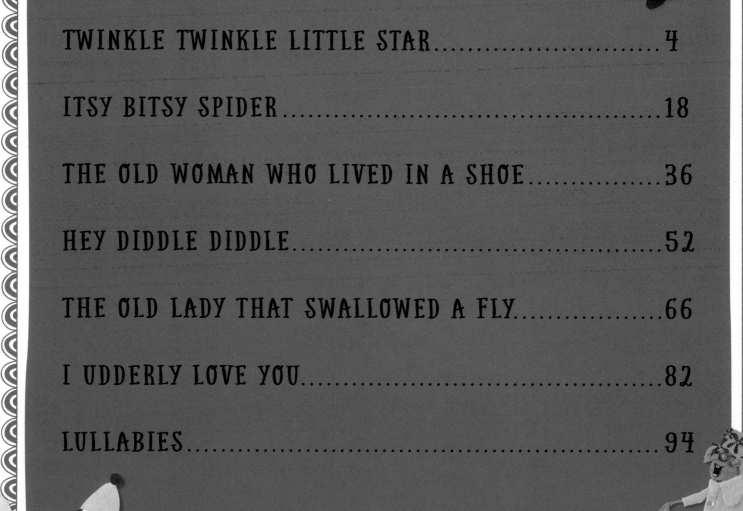

TWINKLE TWINKLE LITTLE STAR

Twinkle, twinkle, little star, how I wonder what you are.

You shine above the world so high, like a lightbulb in the sky.

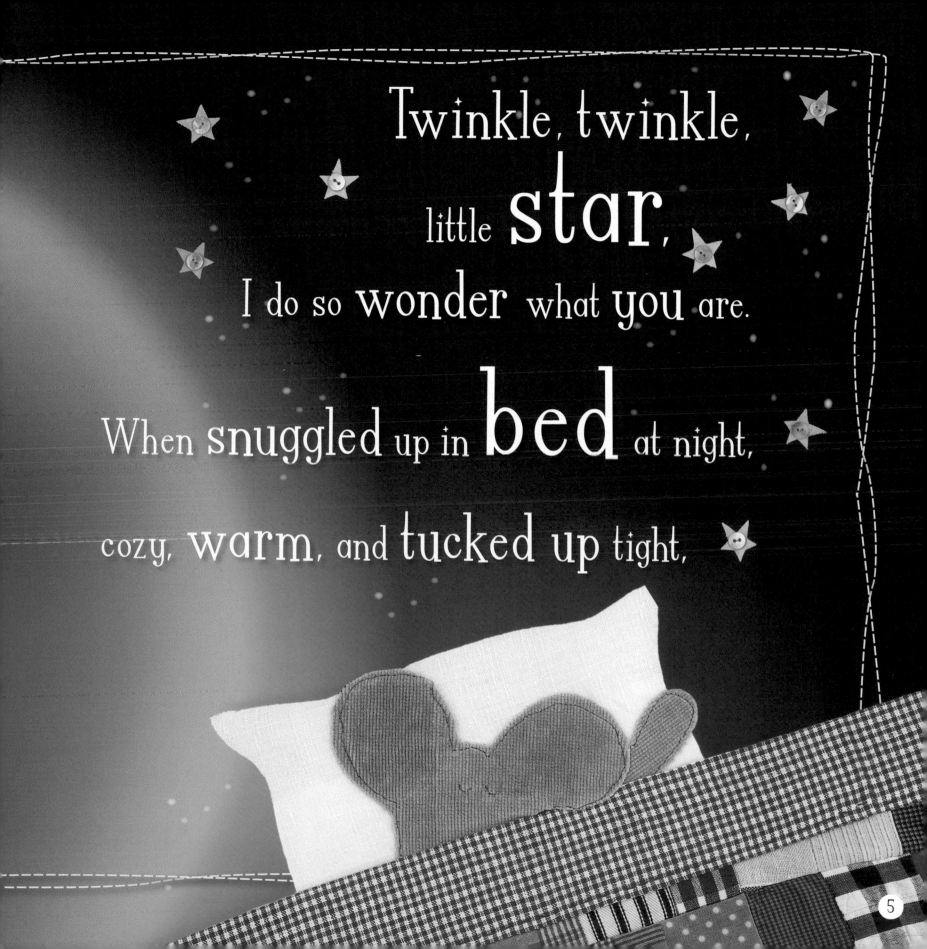

Twinkle, twinkle, little star,
I do so wonder what you are.

When snuggled up in bed at night,
cozy, warm, and tucked up tight,

5

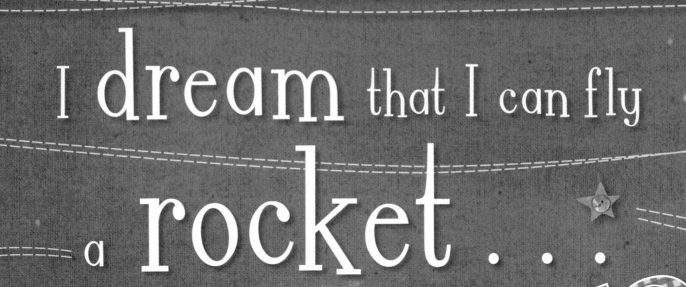

I dream that I can fly
a rocket . . .

5 4 3 2

and gather
stardust in my pocket.

1

Blast off!

7

Twinkle, twinkle, little star,

what do YOU see from afar?

Hello!

¡Hola!

Are there **mice** just like me living way across the **sea**?

Guten Tag!

Bonjour!

Ciao!

Are there **stars** for us all up there?

All mine!

Wheeeeee!

Jump!

Or do some folks have to share?

11

Twinkle, twinkle, little **star**, how I wonder what **you** are!

Wheeeeeeeeee!

I want to be a **star** like you,

and see the **world** the way you do.

Twinkle, twinkle, little star,
how I wonder what you are.

When it's time to climb the stairs,

to **brush** my **teeth**
and say my **prayers**,

through my **window** I can see
that you are **smiling** down on me.

Twinkle, twinkle, little **star**, how I wonder what **you** are.

ITSY BITSY SPIDER

Itsy Bitsy Spider
went UP the waterspout.
DOWN came the rain,
and washed the spider OUT.

Out came the SUN

and dried up all the rain,

so **Itsy Bitsy Spider**

climbed up the spout again.

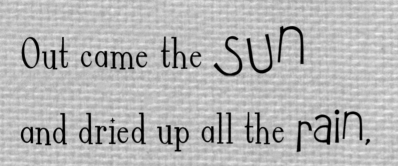

Here we go again!

But why does **Itsy** climb the **spout?**

(In case you are in any doubt.)

Because he's **SPUN** his web up **high,**

so he can **see** the **world** go by . . .

(It's easy **dropping** to the floor,
but climbing **UP** is quite a chore.)

Itsy Bitsy Spider

doesn't like the **rain**,

he's got his **swimming goggles** on,

(he won't get
caught again).

But . . . just as he starts climbing
UP the waterspout,
another shower of rain falls down
and
washes
Itsy
out!

Uh-oh!

23

Now **Itsy's** trying once again,

with his **umbrella** ready,

the **rain** won't beat him **this** time

if he takes it

nice and **steady**.

There **has** to be another way

to get home on a rainy day!

Looking **around**, what's **Itsy** seen?
A **round** and **bouncy** trampoline!

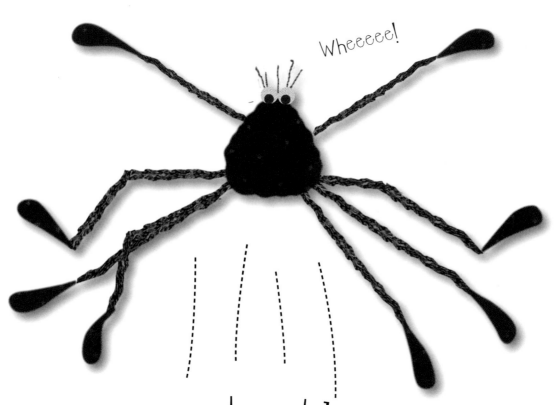

Wheeeee!

He's found a way to get home **fast** . . .

but bounces high

and flies straight past...

Not again!

Over the hedge,

over the wall,

a striped tent

breaks his fall.

Looking puzzled,

Itsy thinks.

He rubs his hairy head and blinks.

27

The **wash** is drying,

the **weather's** fine,

28

Itsy wobbles on the line,

when suddenly a breezy breeze blows Itsy to some nearby trees.

Through the leaves,
Itsy spies
several pairs of
beady eyes.

"But **worse** than that,"
Itsy squeaks,
"a row of **long**
and **pointy** beaks."

Aaaaargh!

Itsy's running,
all puffed out,

but in the distance,

sees the

spout.

31

It's the best idea
he's had all day.
He'll climb the spout
another way.

The rain comes down
inside the spout,

so he'll climb UP
not IN, but OUT!

Back in his web,

he's happy now.

(It's easy when you've worked out how . . .)

The lesson learned?

don't wear a frown –

even when the rain comes down!

Home at last!

So **Itsy Bitsy Spider** can climb the waterspout.

And even if the rain pours down, it can't wash **Itsy** out.

For **Itsy Bitsy Spider** has found another way,

and now it's really easy

Up I go!

to climb the spout all day.

THE OLD WOMAN WHO LIVED IN A SHOE

There was an **old woman** who lived in a shoe,

with so many **children** –

what could they all do?

Every day, they'd have some fun,

but not until

the **chores** were done!

On **Monday,** they have clothes to wash,
and sheets to clean
with a **splish** and a **splosh.**

Spinning around in the **big** machine, the laundry is soon all fresh and clean.

39

On **Tuesday,** every child **must** choose
some **polish** and a pair of shoes.

They **scrape** and **brush** and **polish** hard,
in a **line** out in the yard.

shoe Polish

Later on, they go for a **swim**,
put armbands on, and **JUMP** right in!

They **laugh** and **dive**
and **splash about**

and towels are **ready**
when they get out.

On **Wednesday,** they get on their knees
to pick some **carrots, beans,** and **peas —**
there's lots of **digging,** gathering **berries,**
and **filling bowls** with piles of **cherries!**

Then . . .

It's **music time** for girls and boys,

lots of singing, lots of **noise!**

They **dance** and **sing** and twirl around

and make a really **amazing** sound.

44

On **Thursday,** a trip to the vet's –

to get a **checkup** for the **pets.**

Once they are **home,** they brush the **fur.**

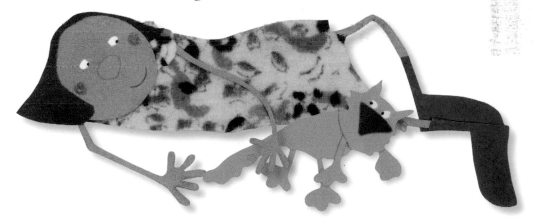

Listen to the kittens **purrr!**

On **Friday,** it's off to the **park** to play –
a **happy** way to spend the day.

A **picnic's** packed, the stroller's full –
and don't forget the **bouncy** ball!

By **Saturday,** the cupboard's bare.
The **old woman** sits in her **chair**

to write a **list** of things they need,
with so many **hungry** mouths to feed!

A **shopping** trip
is quickly planned,
and **everybody**
lends a hand.

Soon the **cart** is
piled up high
with all the things
they need to **buy.**

49

Sunday is the day of rest —
see them in their
Sunday best,

all in a row, **one** by **one**.

Can you **remember**

the **things** they've done?

HEY DIDDLE DIDDLE

Hey diddle diddle, the cat and the fiddle,

the cow
jumps over
the Moon,

the little dog laughs
to see
such fun,

54

and the dish **runs away** with the spoon.

Hey diddle diddle, when Cat plays his fiddle, Dog sings along to the tune,

then Dog starts to **laugh** when Dish comes back with the spoon.

The piggies all prance,

the elephants
dance,

59

the monkeys start softly to croon,

and, hand in hand,
the kangaroos stand,

tapping their toes to the tune!

Hey diddle diddle,
Cat hangs up his fiddle
and Moon looks down from on high.

and everyone's waving
bye-bye,   bye-bye,

and everyone's waving bye-bye.

THE OLD LADY WHO SWALLOWED A FLY

There was an **old lady** who **swallowed** a fly. Why, oh **why**, did she swallow a **fly?**

Oh my, oh my!

Tra la la!

That little old lady was **walking** along,

enjoying the sunshine

and **singing** a song.

When **all of a sudden**

a fly flew south,

and ended up flying right into her **mouth!**

That **poor** old lady – what a to-do!

Imagine if that happened to **you!**

The fly now buzzes and **tickles** her **tummy**
(she didn't think it tasted so yummy)!

But **suddenly** she has an **idea**

to make the naughty fly disappear:

to catch the fly she swallows

a spider –

so now she has them **both** inside her!

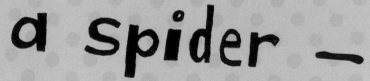

Oh my, oh my!

Down by the pond
she **spots** a **frog**,

sitting still on a **speckled** log.

Without even saying,

"How do you do?"

cRoAK!

she picks up the frog and

swallows

him too!

Feeling just a **little queasy**

(certainly not so bright and breezy),

she **spots** a heron on a nest –

I wonder if **you** can

guess the rest?

How **absurd**. . .
to swallow a **bird**!

Oh my, oh my!

How could she **do** that?
We don't know how —
but you won't **believe**
what happens now . . .

Pretty Kitty sits and **purrs**;
from behind her something **stirs.**

Before **poor puss**
has time
to flee . . .

cREam

she's washed down
with a
cup of **tea!**

Imagine **that,**
to swallow a
cat!

Oh my, oh my!

By this time it's **getting dark.**
Prince the **dog** plays in the park.

But poor old Prince
just does not see
the **old lady**
lurking by a big tree.

GULP!

Poor Prince . . .

The old lady's **tummy** is about to **burst** – she wished she'd thought more **carefully** first.

She swallowed the **dog**

to catch the cat.

She swallowed the **cat**

to catch the bird.

She swallowed the **bird**

to catch the frog.

She swallowed the **frog**

to catch the spider.

She swallowed the **spider**

to catch the fly . . .

if **only** that fly had just **flown by.**

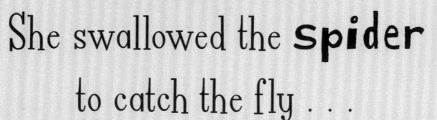

Oh my, oh my!

I UDDERLY LOVE YOU

Udderley
sque-e-eze!
I love
everything about you:
your tail, your ears,
your toes.

82

I love the softness of your skin, your silky, s-moo-th, wet nose.

83

I love your every **moo**-vement,

the way you skip about,

and how your **hooves** point inwards,

while all your **knees** stick out!

I love the way
you chatter,
the funny things you say,
the **moo**-sic
that you sing to me,

the silly games we play.

And when you
go exploring,
it makes me
really proud,

tweet! tweet!

Grrr! Grrr!

DOG

to know you'll always find me,

Moo! Moo! Moo! Moo!

Moo!

Moo!

even in a crowd.

89

At night-time, in the **moo**-nlight, when the stars shine overhead,

I watch you as you're sleeping in your snuggly, little bed.

91

I love you when you're sad.

ha-ha! ha-ha!

I love you when you're happy,

Even when you're **moo**-dy, not meaning to be bad.

NO! NO! NO!

MOO-hoo!

Every day with you is special, I love you through and through,

I UDDERLY, UDDERLY LOVE YOU and I know you love me too!

93

LULLABIES

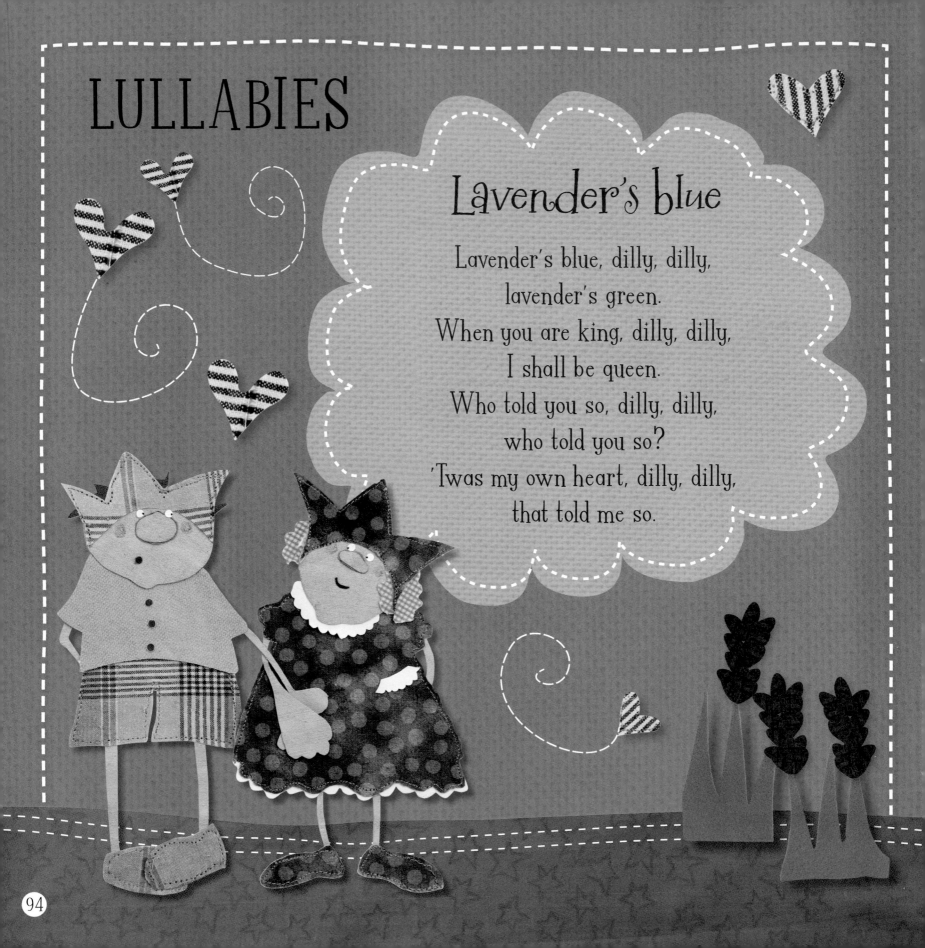

Lavender's blue

Lavender's blue, dilly, dilly,
lavender's green.
When you are king, dilly, dilly,
I shall be queen.
Who told you so, dilly, dilly,
who told you so?
'Twas my own heart, dilly, dilly,
that told me so.

Sleep, Baby, sleep

Sleep, Baby, sleep,
long and safe and deep.
The wind will blow
the dreamland tree
and from it shake
sweet dreams for thee.
Sleep, Baby, sleep,
our cottage vale is deep.
The little lamb
is on the green,
with snowy fleece
so soft and clean.
Sleep, Baby, sleep.

Rock-a-bye, Baby

Rock-a-bye, Baby,
on the treetop.
When the wind blows,
the cradle will rock.
When the bough breaks,
the cradle will fall,
and down will come Baby,
cradle and all.